BASEBALL BLACKOUT

By Ellen Guidone
Illustrated by Duendes del Sur

Hello Reader — Level 1

ISBN 0-439-20233-7

12 11 10 9 8 7 6 5 4 3 2 1   1 2 3 4 5 6

Designed by Maria Stasavage

Printed in the U.S.A.
First Scholastic printing, March 2001

W9-ALU-443

SCHOLASTIC INC.
New York Toronto London Auckland Sydney
Mexico City New Delhi Hong Kong

One night, 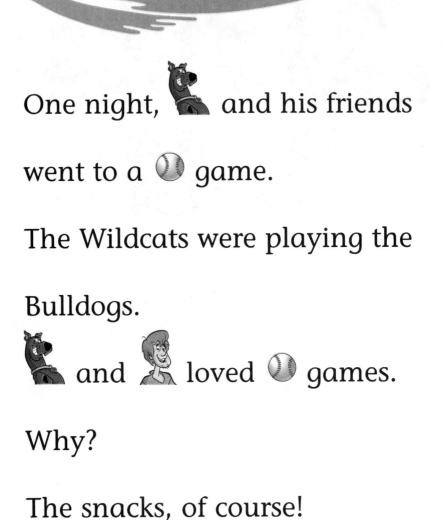 and his friends

went to a ⚾ game.

The Wildcats were playing the

Bulldogs.

and loved ⚾ games.

Why?

The snacks, of course!

, , , and .

Yummy!

, and  watched the

game.

and played their own

game.

 threw up in the air.

 caught them in his mouth!

Suddenly, all the  went out.

"Hey," said. "I cannot find

my !"

"Ree roo!" barked.

turned on a .

The gang heard some players

talking to each other.

"The went out," said one

player. "Now our coach is gone!"

"And our is missing, too!"

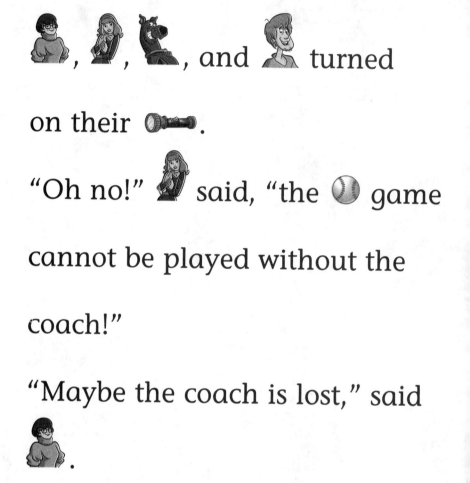

, , , and turned

on their .

"Oh no!" said, "the game

cannot be played without the

coach!"

"Maybe the coach is lost," said

.

"Maybe this stadium is

haunted," said. "Maybe a

took the coach and the ."

 and took a . They

went to the snack bar.

"Let's search for clues in the

," said , "and in the ."

"Rokay!" barked .

"Then we can check the

and the !" said.

They did not find any clues in

the .

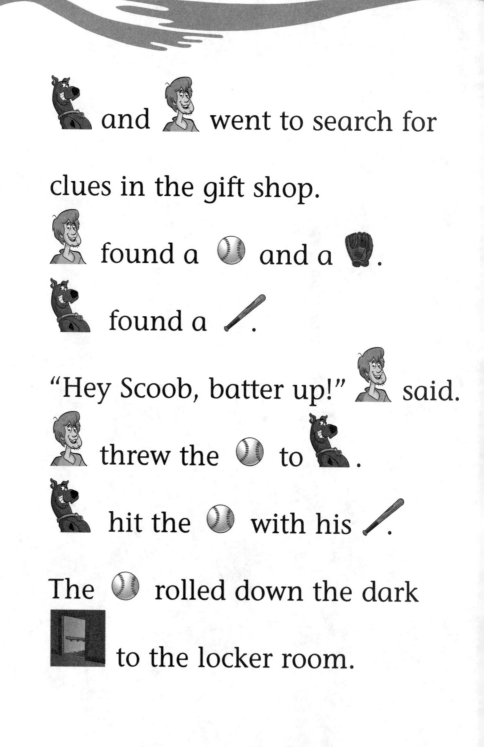

and went to search for clues in the gift shop.

found a and a .

found a .

"Hey Scoob, batter up!" said.

threw the to .

hit the with his .

The rolled down the dark to the locker room.

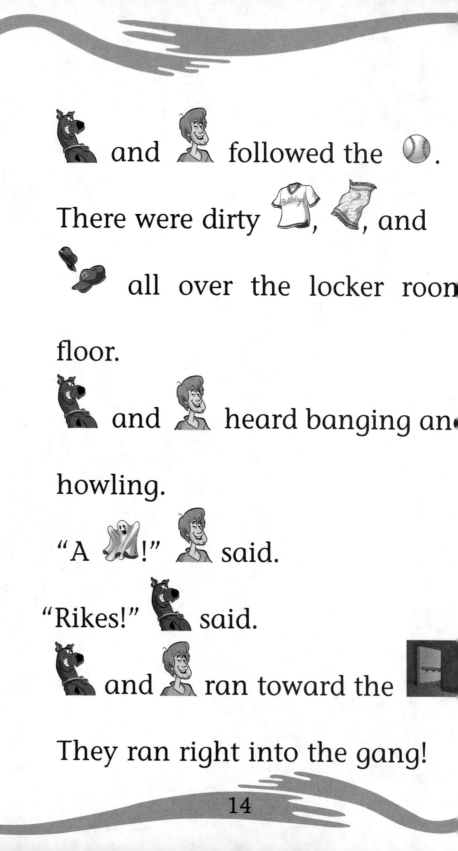

and followed the .

There were dirty , , and

all over the locker room

floor.

and heard banging and

howling.

"A !" said.

"Rikes!" said.

and ran toward the

They ran right into the gang!

"We found a 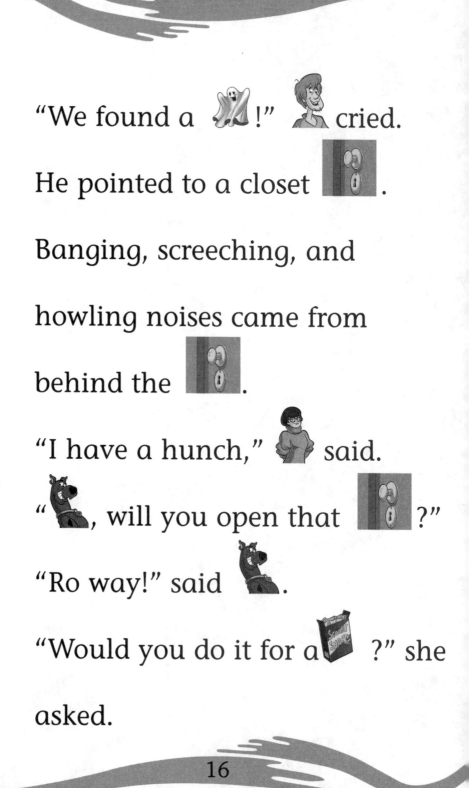!" cried.

He pointed to a closet.

Banging, screeching, and

howling noises came from

behind the.

"I have a hunch," said.

", will you open that ?"

"Ro way!" said.

"Would you do it for a ?" she

asked.

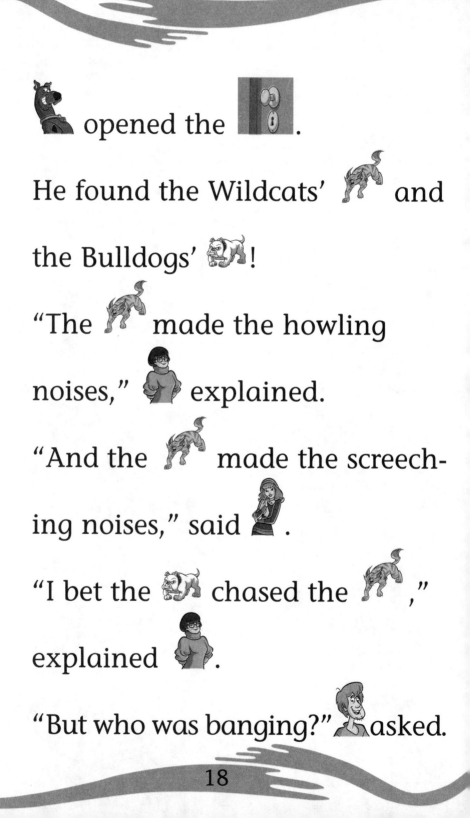 opened the [door].

He found the Wildcats' [wildcat] and the Bulldogs' [bulldog]!

"The [wildcat] made the howling noises," [Velma] explained.

"And the [wildcat] made the screeching noises," said [Daphne].

"I bet the [bulldog] chased the [wildcat]," explained [Velma].

"But who was banging?" [Shaggy] asked.

"I was," said the coach. He

stepped through the .

"I came down here to turn the

back on," the coach said.

"But the and chased me

into this closet. It was too dark.

I could not find the . Then

opened the . Thank

you, ."

" saved the 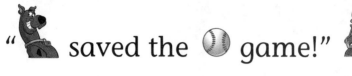 game!" said.

 picked up a 🏏.

He swung the 🏏 like a ⚾ player.

"I think 🐕 is ready to play!" said.

"Scooby Dooby Doo!" barked.

Did you spot all the picture clues in this Scooby-Doo mystery?

Each picture clue is on a flash card. Ask a grown-up to cut out the flash cards. Then try reading the words on the back of the cards. The pictures will be your clue.

Reading is fun with Scooby-Doo!